CHL

W9-BJU-397

jW 752 gh
Wise   3.95
    The ghost town monster

CHILDREN'S LIBRARY

DENVER
PUBLIC LIBRARY

FINE FOR OVERTIME

DEMCO

R01107 27029

GHOST TOWN MONSTER

GHOST TOWN MONSTER

By
Robert Wise

Illustrations By
Paul Snyder

DENVER
PUBLIC LIBRARY

JUN 76

CITY & COUNTY OF DENVER

EMC CORPORATION
ST. PAUL, MINNESOTA

G672610

R01107 27029

Library of Congress Cataloging in Publication Data

Wise, Robert A
    The ghost town monster.

    (His Sea Wolf mysteries)
    SUMMARY: Although none of them believe in ghosts or
monsters, four youngsters and their Indian guide begin
to get nervous when they find strange large footprints
around their camp.
    [1. Mystery and detective stories] I. Snyder,
Paul, 1923-   illus. II. Title.
PZ7.W777Gh   [Fic]   74-16076
ISBN 0-88436-142-X (lib. bdg.)
ISBN 0-88436-143-8 (pbk.)

Copyright 1974 by EMC Corporation
All rights reserved. Published 1974

No part of this publication can be
reproduced, stored in a retrieval
system, or transmitted in any form
or by any means; electronic, mechanical,
photocopying, recording, or otherwise,
without the permission of the publisher.

Published by EMC Corporation
180 East Sixth Street
St. Paul, Minnesota 55101
Printed in the United States of America
0 9 8 7 6 5 4 3 2 1

JW
752
gh

SEA WOLF MYSTERIES

Johnny Goodfire moored his boat, the *Sea Wolf*, among some old pilings. "Used to be a logging camp here," he said. "This was a dock for the old lumber ships. But there's nothing left now except old pilings."

"How do we get to shore?" asked Cindy.

"We take the dinghy," said Johnny. "I'll row you and Eddie to shore. Then we'll load the backpacks. Next will be Karen and Ron. Then we're on our way to the ghost town."

"This is going to be fun," said Cindy to Karen when they had all stepped ashore. "I'm glad I could spend two weeks with you and your brother."

6

"Well," said Karen, "Ron and I were lucky to spend the summer on Hawk Island."

"And to have a pal like Johnny," Ron added.

Their Indian friend said, "Now this is the mainland of British Columbia. We'll have to pack in from here."

"Is it a long walk to the ghost town?" asked Karen.

"It's a couple of miles," said Johnny. "But the trail is pretty good in most places."

"What's the name of that town again?" asked Eddie.

"Riverport. It's right on Carpenter Creek. It used to be a busy mining town. Then the gold ran out and all the people left. There was nothing to keep them there anymore."

The sun was shining brightly through the trees. There was a wonderful smell of cedar in the summer air. They all headed up the path carrying their gear in their backpacks.

8

In a little while the path got steeper. "This is great," said Cindy as they hiked up the trail. "I don't know about that," laughed Ron. "These backpacks get heavier with every step."

"You're a sissy," teased Johnny Goodfire.

"I'm already getting sunburned," croaked Eddie, who was blond and fair.

"Well, Cindy will have freckles on her freckles," laughed Karen.

Cindy stopped and pointed. "Oh, look at the little waterfall over there! Wouldn't it be great to stand under it and get cooled off?"

"No," warned Johnny. "If I remember right, a demon lives there. And in the cave behind the waterfall lives a great bird with a sharp beak. He likes to eat people." Johnny winked at Karen.

"Well, then," said Cindy, who took Johnny's monster stories with a grain of salt, "if we can't cool off in the waterfall, I wish we could be at the top of that mountain." She pointed to a distant peak in the mountain range ahead of them. "We could cool off in the snow!"

"We could only go as far as the snow line and no farther," said Johnny Goodfire. "The great Thunderbird lives beyond. He wouldn't want to be disturbed. He would be angry."

10

"Why?" asked Karen.

"All I know," said Johnny, "is that once when the world was younger, some Indians climbed the mountain. Thunderbird sent fire and rocks down the side of the mountain."

"That was a volcano," said Eddie.

"Thunderbird caused it," insisted Johnny.

"Johnny," said Ron, "you're kidding us."

"My people tell the stories," said Johnny. "And my grandfather as a boy heard that story from the chief of our tribe. The old wise people believe the stories that were handed down. Why shouldn't we?" asked Johnny with a smile.

The explorers trudged on, taking in the sights around them. They finally arrived at the ghost town in time for a late lunch.

Johnny and Eddie lingered over their meal. Cindy was a city girl, not used to hiking. She took a nap.

Karen and Ron exchanged looks. "Let's explore," suggested Ron. Karen nodded excitedly.

First they headed for the old grocery store with the false front. They went inside. The shelves were empty and the windows were broken out.

Karen ran behind the counter. "Just imagine how it must have been!"

"Howdy there, ma'am," said Ron in his deepest voice. "I'll take a pound of bacon and some beans."

"What kind of beans?"

"Jelly beans!"

Laughing, they ran out and over to the saloon next door. As they walked through the batwing doors one of the rusty hinges broke. "I'm Calamity Jane and I'll have some red eye," said Karen.

"Smile when you say that, stranger," growled Ron. They both reached for imaginary sixguns. Ron hit the dust gasping, "You got me Calamity."

They ran to the old, three-story hotel and walked up to the desk. "Young man," said Karen, "I'm the new school teacher. I'll have a room overlooking the river." They turned and ran upstairs.

They peeked out of a broken window and saw Eddie and Cindy coming.

"I wondered how long it would be," laughed Karen.

"Yeah, I figured they'd come looking for us," said Ron. "Hey, let's scare 'em."

They waited just out of sight at the head of the stairs until Eddie and Cindy came in. Then they began to moan loudly.

"What's *that?*" they heard Cindy ask nervously.

"Oh, it's just Ron and Karen," snorted Eddie. "And we were going to tell them about something *really odd* that we found."

Karen and Ron came tumbling downstairs. "We'll be good," promised Karen. "Tell us what you found."

"Okay," said Cindy, "follow us."

They led Karen and Ron to a deserted house at the end of the street. It was like all the rest inside — dusty, falling apart, and the windows broken.

"So?" asked Karen.

"Well, don't you notice something?" asked Cindy.

Ron and Karen looked around. "Well, it seems a little cleaner," said Karen. "Like it might have been swept out."

"No cobwebs," noticed Ron. "No broken glass lying around."

"And something else," said Eddie.

Karen and Ron were puzzled.

"It's a kind of a smell," said Cindy.

Karen nodded. "Yes, the others smelled damp and musty. But this place smells different. Like there might have been a fire in that old potbelly stove over there and things dried out."

Ron sniffed the air. "There's something else," he said. He sniffed again.

"What else?" asked Eddie, sniffing too.

"Well, Dad smokes a pipe," Ron said. "And it kind of reminds me of that. Like the stale, sweet smell of pipe tobacco."

"You're right," agreed Karen.

Eddie went over to the stove and opened the iron door.

"There are ashes in here. But I can't tell how old they are."

16

"Johnny might know," said Ron.

"Where is Johnny?" asked Karen.

"Fishing," said Eddie.

"Well," said Cindy, "maybe we're making too much of this. What if somebody did come by here and stay overnight?"

"It's just that this town is way up in the wilderness," said Eddie. Who could have been here? Nobody knows about this place."

"Johnny does," said Cindy.

"Yes," said Eddie, "but Johnny is special."

"The old freight wagon road to the town is grown over," said Ron. "And you'd have to come by trail from the old logging camp."

"Maybe there's another trail in," insisted Cindy. "One we don't know about."

"That could be," said Eddie.

They all walked out into the late afternoon sunshine. Johnny was setting up pup tents in the middle of the street, across from the old hotel.

"We'll have a nice campfire and cook our dinner in that grassy area down by the river," said Johnny. "But if there's a flash flood, that river could rise during the night. I thought we'd like to sleep here."

18

"What's the matter with the hotel?" asked Eddie.

"Fine," grinned Johnny, "if you want to sleep inside on the hard floor with the spiders and other crawly things. Me, I want to sleep in the fresh air under the stars."

"Me too!" answered the others.

Johnny held up a string of three trout. "Look. While you guys were fooling around I caught our supper. Only we need a couple more."

Karen and Ron were already fumbling in their packs for some light tackle they had brought. While they fished, Johnny got a campfire started. Eddie and Cindy gathered wood.

Karen and Ron exchanged smiles when they heard Cindy scold Johnny. "You certainly are a bad fire builder. They named you wrong, Johnny Goodfire!"

The group had a good hot meal as the sun set behind the old ghost town. Johnny sat telling about Indian demons and monsters as the shadows lengthened. Everyone was getting nervous. Eddie kept looking over his shoulder.

Karen and Ron exchanged mischievous looks and slipped away in the shadows. "We'll give 'em a good scare this time," snickered Ron.

They entered an old building and stood in the dark window.

"Oh, I wish I had a white sheet to wrap around us," whispered Karen, and both smothered their mirth. Together they gave a low howl.

21

Cindy and Eddie gave little shrieks. Even Johnny jumped. It was getting spooky in the old ghost town.

"Ron and Karen!" cried Cindy. "That was a dirty trick!"

They laughed and made a move to return to camp. Suddenly Karen grabbed Ron's arm. "I heard a funny sound behind us!" she whispered.

Ron turned. He thought he saw a big shadowy figure move to the back of the building.

They stood rooted with fright. There was a sound like rusty hinges creaking. Then they thought they heard a door closing.

"It went out the back door," whispered Ron.

"What was it?"

"I don't know. It was big and black."

"It's not Johnny," said Karen. "I can see him sitting by the fire."

22

They broke into a run back to camp.

Johnny saw their white faces and laughed. "You two scared yourselves more than you did us."

"No!" said Ron. "There was something big and black in there!"

Eddie and Cindy broke into fits of laughter.

"Maybe it was one of your Indian monsters," said Ron seriously.

Johnny shook his head. "They live in caves, lakes, and waterfalls — not in ghost towns!"

Cindy began to sing. Johnny and Eddie joined in and soon Karen and Ron did too. Ron looked at his sister and shrugged. It was a spooky place. Maybe they were just jumping at shadows.

The group was tired from the long hike. Soon they were stretched out in their sleeping bags looking at the stars overhead.

Something woke Ron out of a bad dream. It was early morning. There had been a crash or a bang. It echoed in his brain. But it was a bright, pretty morning. Birds were singing. The river made a splashing sound.

The noise had been part of his bad dream, Ron decided. He looked around. Eddie and the girls were still asleep. But Johnny Goodfire's sleeping bag was empty.

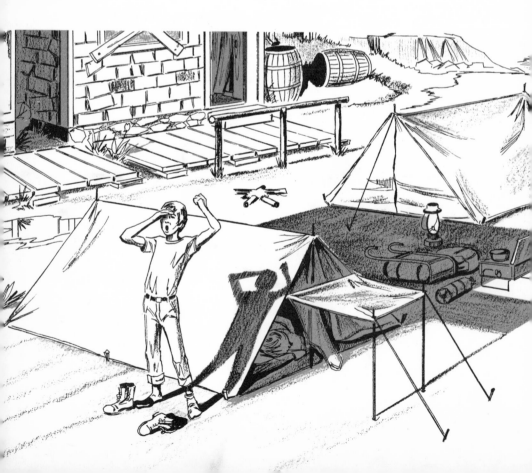

Ron found Johnny near the edge of town. The Indian was kneeling at the edge of the town's single dirt street.

"Was that you making all the noise?" asked Ron.

"Something wake you too?" asked Johnny. He motioned at the ground. "Look. Footprints. They weren't here yesterday."

"Are they from some animal?" asked Ron, kneeling beside him.

DENVER
PUBLIC LIBRARY

JUN '76

CITY & COUNTY OF DENVER

"I can't tell," said Johnny. "There isn't a full print here. But this wasn't made by any shoe."

Karen came running. "Eddie and Cindy are fixing breakfast!"

"Okay," said Johnny. "Let's go back and eat. Then I want to follow those tracks. We want to get a look at the old mine, anyhow, before we head back."

Karen stared at the print in the dust. "Maybe it was a bear?" she asked.

"No bear," said Johnny firmly.

Cindy and Eddie were excited when they got back. "There were some raccoons down by the river," said Cindy. "They're so cute!"

"And a deer came right into camp," said Eddie.

They ate quickly and followed Johnny back to the edge of town. Soon he was following the tracks.

Then he stopped. "Holy cow!" he said. "Will you look at that footprint!"

"It's huge!" gasped Cindy.

"Bigfoot," said Johnny. "It's a big hairy monster that lives in caves. Indians call him Bigfoot."

"Johnny, you and your Indian demons," said Cindy.

"This one is very real," said Johnny. "We'd better get back and break camp. It's a long hike back to the *Sea Wolf*."

"But what about the old gold mine," said Ron. "We were going to see the mine before we left."

"Those footprints lead right to it," said Johnny. "And Bigfoot likes to live in caves. He could be in the mine."

"I don't believe in Bigfoot," said Cindy. "Karen and Ron made that footprint somehow. They're always trying to scare us."

Karen and Ron exchanged startled looks.

"It's phony," agreed Eddie. "You guys! Think I'll go back and coax that deer up." Eddie was a sucker for anything with four feet.

"Well, Johnny, can Karen and I go to the top of that little hill?" asked Ron. "Maybe we can see the mine from a distance."

"Yes," said Karen. "And I want to look for old bottles."

"Okay, you guys," said Johnny. "I'll give you about ten minutes! Then you hustle back to camp."

Ron and Karen broke into a run toward the hill.

"Don't go near that mine!" Johnny shouted. "It's dangerous. Even if there isn't a Bigfoot hanging around."

From the top of the hill Karen and Ron could see the mine — a dark tunnel in the side of a hill. Karen looked at Ron. "Should we? We might never get another chance."

"Maybe just a peek inside," said Ron. "Come on, sis. Hurry!"

"I brought a flashlight," said Karen. "I shoved it into my pocket at breakfast. That's when Johnny said we'd go take a look at the old mine."

"Yeah," said Ron, "before he saw those Bigfoot footprints. You know, I have the feeling I've seen prints like that before."

"In a nightmare," shuddered Karen. "Over there's the mine entrance."

"Look!" said Ron. They were staring at more big prints. "They go over back of the mine," said Ron. "So we know he's not inside."

"You think there is a Bigfoot?" asked Karen.

"No," said Ron.

"I don't know," said Karen. "Johnny's told us about so many Indian demons, monsters, and evil spirits that I'm beginning to believe in them."

"They're legends," said Ron. "Tall tales handed down from mouth to mouth at campfires to kill a winter evening."

"Those footprints are real," Karen reminded him.

"It's a mystery," said Ron. "But I still don't think they belong to Bigfoot. Here's the mine entrance."

"Let's take a quick look," said Karen.

They walked inside the entrance and down the mine tunnel. Karen was scared. She wanted to bolt and run. She looked at Ron in the semi-darkness. All she could see was the whites of his eyes.

They kept going. Karen used her flashlight. The timbers overhead creaked and groaned. Karen turned her light toward the ceiling.

"Those old timber supports have been here over a hundred years," said Ron. "They look all rotten. Like they're about to give away."

"A couple of beams look like they're split," said Karen. "Well, we've seen it, let's hit for camp before Johnny comes after us."

"Look," said Ron, pointing to an opening.

"Looks different than the mine tunnel," said Karen.

"It's a cave," said Ron. "I'll bet the gold was discovered first in the cave. And they built the mine around it."

"Let's take a quick look," suggested Karen.

As they turned toward the cave, there was a noise behind them. Karen swung her light, which was beginning to get dim now. The beam picked up small red eyes.

"A big rat!" said Ron. "Wow, I thought it was Bigfoot!"

He picked up the largest rock he could find and heaved it. His aim was poor. The rock hit one of the support beams.

There was a loud creaking and groaning from the timber. Then the beam split under the weight of the ceiling. With a rumbling roar the whole ceiling of the mine collapsed. Karen and Ron ran for the cave. They choked on the dust.

"The entrance is blocked," gasped Karen. "We'll never get out!"

Ron could only stand rooted, his mouth dry, his heart pounding.

"You think Johnny heard the cave-in?" asked Karen in a thin, frightened voice.

"No, we're too far away," said Ron. "And I doubt if he could dig us out if he did. We've got to find another way out!"

They moved deeper into the cave. Karen's flashlight was flickering and the light was beginning to go orange.

"Wish you had put fresh batteries in that thing," said Ron.

"I smell fresh air!" yelled Karen.

It seemed to be coming from a small tunnel-like hole up on a ledge, just over their heads. Ron scrambled up and Karen came close behind.

"Looks like a long tunnel or passageway," said Ron. "We'll have to crawl." He turned the flashlight into the passageway. "Can't see anything." He gave the flashlight a shake and the light went out.

"Oh great," groaned Ron. He fought down panic. It was pitch black.

"There's fresh air coming from here," Karen insisted.

"Come on then," said Ron. "We've got no other choice!"

They crawled on their hands and knees. But the passageway lowered. Soon they had to crawl flat on their stomachs. Ron broke into a sweat. His heart was pounding. Karen was breathing hard.

"There's another passageway that branches off here," gasped Ron.

"Keep going," said Karen.

But soon the solid rock was pressing down on them.

"It narrows," said Ron. "We gotta go back!"

They slid backward until they came to the Y. "Go the other way!" said Karen.

It seemed like there was more air. Then the tunnel began to slant down. It was getting steeper. Ron's heart was in his mouth. They began to slide. Faster! They were sliding head first out of control.

Then they were falling. This is it, thought Ron. They hit water with a splash.

They looked up, spitting water. There was daylight overhead. But it was out of reach.

Ron saw it first. A ladder! But something was coming down the ladder. Something with big feet.

Then Karen let out a cry of relief. It was a man in a black rubber wet suit. He had flippers on his feet.

The young man had curly red hair and a big grin. "Come on, you two. Let's get you up into the sunshine!"

Karen and Ron were soon drying out under a blue sky.

"I've been exploring some of the underground passages with scuba gear," the man explained. My name's Dave Edwards. Thought I might find some gold, but no luck."

"How'd you get up to this old ghost town?" asked Ron.

"By Jeep. There's a trail just the other side of the ghost town. I'm camped there."

"I knew I recognized those footprints from somewhere," said Ron.

"Sorry if I shook you guys up," said David. "At first I resented you being here. I guess I thought the five of you were after gold too. Then when I saw you two scaring the rest, on impulse I decided to get into the act."

"I guess those 'monster' tracks would have kept us from ever coming back again," said Karen.

"Well, I was going to introduce myself before you left camp," said Dave.

Ron suddenly broke into a broad grin. "Hey," he said, "I know an Indian pal of ours who believes in monsters!"

The three of them grinned. They walked back to the ghost town. Johnny Goodfire was packing the camp gear. Eddie and Cindy were off trying to coax up the deer.

Johnny let out a yelp when a wet black flipper touched his cheek from behind. And Karen and Ron rolled on the ground, holding their sides with laughter.